Snowflake Hollow - Part 8

12 Days of Christmas, Volume 8

Lexy Timms

Published by Dark Shadow Publishing, 2021.

SNOWFLAKE HOLLOW - PART 8

First edition. December 8, 2021.

Written by Lexy Timms.

SNOWFLAKE HOLLOW

12 DAYS OF CHRISTMAS
PART EIGHT

USA TODAY BESTSELLING AUTHOR

LEXY TIMMS

Copyright 2021 By LEXY TIMMS

Snowflake
HOLLOW
12 DAYS OF CHRISTMAS
PART EIGHT
USA TODAY BESTSELLING AUTHOR
LEXY TIMMS

All rights reserved.
Snow Flake Hollow
~ Part 8 ~
12 Days of Christmas Series
Copyright 2021 by Lexy Timms
Cover by: **Book Cover by Design**[1]

---

1. http://bookcoverbydesign.co.uk/

12 Days of Christmas Series

Find Lexy Timms:

LEXY TIMMS NEWSLETTER:
https://www.lexytimms.com/newsletter
Lexy Timms Facebook Page:
https://www.facebook.com/SavingForever
Lexy Timms Website:
http://www.lexytimms.com

Want to read more...
For **FREE**?
Sign up for Lexy Timms' newsletter
And she'll send you updates on new releases, ARC copies of books and
a whole lotta fun!
Sign up for news and updates!
https://www.lexytimms.com/newsletter

Snow Flake Hollow

LEAVE A LITTLE SPARKLE wherever you go…

She's not the biggest fan of Christmas – which is akin to a major sin in the little town of Snowflake Hollow. And with a name like Holly White, it's fitting that she owns the only B&B in town. The whole season is a huge deal, and the people coming to stay at the B&B are paying a premium to get the ultimate festive experience. She's trying to keep the guests busy, but Hank the Handyman just broke his leg trying to hang the lights. Now she has to figure out how to make the holiday festivities happen all by herself.

Enter Lawson Lane.

Mister tall, dark and handsome, has come home to see his mother over the holidays, and is surprised to see Holly as the owner of the B&B.

When he notices her struggling to get things done, he offers a helping hand. Seeing Holly again and enjoying the holidays might take a Christmas miracle—or he might end up with a lump of coal in his stocking.

It's 12 days of festive fun, what could possibly go wrong?

Lexy Timms brings you a Christmas holiday romance with 12 days of Christmas – each part of the story releasing like opening an advent calendar! Join in the holiday spirit with a festive read and some laughs to get you into the Christmas season.

Chapter Forty-Three

Lawson

THE GLASS OF EGGNOG spiked with rum I had the night before didn't really have any impact on me, so I didn't have any trouble getting up early the next morning. I had a feeling I was going to be one of the few adults in the place who was going to be able to say that, including good old Nancy. She might have started the night with a sour face and a judgmental attitude, but a couple of pours of rum later, she was out of that chair and rocking around the Christmas tree.

Holly, on the other hand, was going to have all kinds of trouble getting herself out of bed and facing the day. I'd seen her drink on a few occasions, but she hadn't gotten ranting at whoever might be around to hear it drunk. Maybe I was mistaken since in the greater scheme of things I hadn't been around her all that much, but I didn't feel like she got drunk like that very often.

The alcohol she poured with increasing generosity into her cup made the eggnog drinkable for her, and it definitely loosened up her tongue, her brain, and all the inhibitions she might have had going into the night. But I could imagine it was probably going to be doing a number on her just as soon as she opened her eyes and the reality of daybreak got to her.

That was why I decided to forego a bit more sleep that morning and head into the kitchen to get the coffee started before she even got up. I'd seen my fair share of people who were suffering the aftermath of a holiday party gone wrong. I'd been that person a time or two. It wasn't pretty. There was a whole lot of jingling of bells and festive merrymaking going on, and knocking back a few spiked eggnogs absolutely made the emptiness under the mistletoe easier to bear in the moment.

Come the next morning, though, it all came back and brought along with it its good friends raging headache, nausea, and regret about a variety of decisions.

There wasn't a whole lot I was going to be able to do to help Holly with whatever was waiting for her on this side of consciousness, but at least the coffee would help some. I got the first pot brewed and into the carafe, and while the second was starting up, I surveyed the kitchen, trying to decide if there was anything I could do to help get breakfast on the table.

I didn't know what Holly might have planned for the meal, but I figured I could get something going for her. I pulled out a couple of loaves of bread and went to the refrigerator for eggs, milk, and cream leftover from making the eggnog the day before. Searching the pantry, I found a couple of cans of pureed pumpkin and set them on the counter.

Holly's biggest mixing bowl was the perfect size for mixing up the basic custard and stirring in the pumpkin. I added brown sugar, maple syrup, and spices, filling the kitchen with the wonderful smell. Cutting thick slices of the bread, I got some soaking up the custard and took out a cast-iron griddle to heat it on the stove.

I had just smothered the hot surface of the griddle with butter and had the first batch of bread turning into my mother's famous pumpkin spice french toast when the door opened and Holly dragged into the room. She looked a little worse for wear and didn't say anything as she crossed the room to the coffee. I couldn't help but giggle as she poured herself a cup almost in slow motion. She took down a gulp black and cringed, likely at the combination of the flavor and the heat.

She didn't acknowledge me as she filled the cup again and this time added some cream and sugar. She stood in silence, staring in the general direction of the kitchen window, but I wasn't sure she was actually seeing anything. That eggnog had definitely gotten to her.

I decided to give her a few moments to get herself together and went to the stove to flip the toast. By the time they were finished and the slices that had been soaking while they cooked were on their way to being toast, I was starting to worry. I really hoped Holly remembered the conversation we had the night before and we hadn't just gone back to the beginning of the silent treatment.

When she was halfway through her third cup of coffee, she looked down into it, then looked over at me.

"Am I drinking pumpkin coffee?" she asked in a slow half whisper.

I let out a chuckle. "No. I'm making pumpkin french toast."

She nodded, then looked over at me slowly. "Why?"

"Because even hungover, you still own a bed-and-breakfast and are going to have guests expecting the aforementioned breakfast when they manage to get up. Granted, judging by your current condition, that might be a bit later than usual," I said.

Holly managed to glare at me. She looked like she was mustering up something to say but eventually just settled on "Shut up."

I laughed and guided her over to the stool next to the table to the side of the kitchen.

"Don't worry about it," I said. "I've been there. You should have seen me at the office Christmas party when one of the guys started doling out Santa's Nipples."

She shot me a look. "I don't want to know what that means."

I eased her down and moved her coffee mug closer to her. "It's a cocktail. Well, it was that night. I'm not entirely sure what it actually was. I'm sure it has a different name in the real world. That night, it was Santa's Nipples. They were served right alongside Elf on the Beach and Blue Reindeer."

Holly shook her head, looking slightly green around the edges. "That doesn't make it any better."

I put the next batch of toast on the platter and brought it out to the dining room with butter and syrup. The usual fruit basket and the carafe of coffee with cream and sugar would be enough to get them started. I went back into the kitchen and found Holly working on a pot of oatmeal and some eggs.

"It's alright," I said. "I got this."

"You don't need to do it all," she said. "I can do something."

"I noticed you cleaned my room."

She looked over at me, the expression in her eyes telling me she knew the significance of that went beyond just having the linens and towels gone and fresh sheets sitting on my bed. Our gaze held for a few seconds, and she nodded.

"I know."

"I'll finish breakfast."

She stepped back from the stove and gestured to the pot, relinquishing control over it. She remembered the conversation.

I finished getting breakfast out on the table for the guests, realizing even more now that I didn't feel like one of them. It wasn't that it would be a bad thing to be a guest at the bed-and-breakfast. It wouldn't be the first time I was. But from the moment I saw Holly again, I felt like I was there for her. I wasn't just staying at the White Christmas Inn because it was the only option in the situation I was in. It wasn't a coincidence I ended up there. I was there for Holly.

When I got back into the kitchen, Holly had gotten two plates out of the cabinet and was filling them with french toast and fruit.

"Thanks," I said. "Want to go outside? It's cold, but it's a pretty morning."

She nodded. "I'll get the plates. You grab more coffee."

"Don't you think you've had enough?" I asked. She glared at me, and I laughed. "I'll get the coffee."

When she had the jitters later, I'd happily hold her until she stopped shaking.

We went out onto the porch, and I immediately got the outdoor heater going. Even if we were only out there for a little while, that extra heat would make it a lot more comfortable. We sat down, and Holly took her first bite of the toast. She let out a little groan, and I smiled.

"This is delicious," she said. "Where did you learn to make it?"

"You like it?" I asked. "It's my mother's recipe. It's one of the things she always used to make during the Christmas season. My father loved it. He used to take pieces of it and build them up into a Christmas tree shape and then drizzle the syrup over it so it would drip like garlands. Sometimes he would add spiced pecans so they were like ornaments."

Holly paused midbite and stared at me. "You do realize you sound like a movie, right? Like, none of this sounds even vaguely real."

She gestured at me with her fork, and I grinned, shrugging as I added some extra syrup to my plate.

"They really got into Christmas," I said. "And kind of everything else. They were the most alive people I've ever known."

I felt a lump in my throat and tried to cough it away, but it stayed firmly lodged even through a sip of coffee and a bite of toast.

"You can tell me it's none of my business and I'll drop it, but can I ask you what's really going on with your mother? I know you gave me the basics of it, but I just don't understand what happened. You talk about the three of you like you were all joined at the hip, then your father died and your mother left town. I don't understand how that all ended with the way things are now." She held up her hands like she was trying to show me she was completely innocent. "Again, you can absolutely tell me to shut up."

I shook my head. "No, it's fine. It's not like it's a big secret. And of all people, I'd like to be able to talk to you about it." I noticed the hint of pink come to her cheeks and felt my heart swell. "My parents were inseparable essentially their whole lives. They loved each other more than

I used to think was possible. When my father died, it made it so much harder for my mother to get through every day. She wanted to be happy because she knew that was what he would have wanted, but she just couldn't do it.

"She convinced herself she needed something different and that if she was away from what they always shared, it would be easier to move forward. It worked for a while. At least, that was what she said. She started a new life, and we spent time together away from Snowflake Hollow. But then more time passed, and she realized she wasn't really living the life she actually wanted. There were things she was doing that she enjoyed, but she wasn't happy, and she missed her life here far too much.

"She didn't sell the house because she couldn't bear to part with it. I know she always felt in her heart that she would end up back here one day."

"So much for you can't come home again," Holly said.

I shook my head. "I've never believed that was true. Of course, you can come home. That is the one thing in this life you can do. No matter what or where or who home is, no matter where you are in life or what is going on with you, if you need peace and comfort, you can always go back. That's where you find yourself again."

"I guess I never really thought of it that way," she said.

"My mother did. Even when I was little, she would tell me she knew one day I was going to grow up and go off on my own. I'd find the career I wanted and make my own life somewhere. But that no matter what, I could always come back home, and she would always be there for me. And I tried to always be there for her, too.

"I tried to take care of her and make sure she always had everything she needed. When she came back here, I figured it was just because she wanted to be comfortable and around the people and places she loved. She didn't tell me it was because she'd started dealing with some health issues that were making her reevaluate life. I hate even saying that. It's not what I want to think about," I said.

"Of course it's not," Holly said. "And that's probably why she didn't tell you."

"But I wish she had. If she told me, I'd have been able to do more. I'd have been able to help her. I'd gotten so wrapped up in my company and building it that I didn't go see her anywhere near as much as I should have. And when we talked, it was probably far shallower and more inconsequential than it should have been. But I never wanted to upset her, and she always sounded fine.

"Then all of a sudden, I found out she'd sold the house, moved into an assisted living facility, and needed me to come sort everything out for her. It was such a shock. I felt horrible."

"There was no reason for you to feel horrible," Holly said. "She made a decision about how she wanted to handle the situation. Remember, you might be the super-successful entrepreneur and everything, but she is still your mother. You are her baby, and she will always want to take care of you. Even if that means going through really challenging times by herself because she doesn't want to upset you."

"And because she wants the control," I said with a half laugh. "She likes to live on her own terms. She doesn't like when I try to make decisions for her or change what she thinks about something."

Holly nodded. "I can definitely see that about Gloria."

We laughed for a few seconds before I let out a sigh. "Anyway, that's what happened. She left Snowflake Hollow because she didn't want to be around the reminders of my father, only to return because she couldn't bear to be away from that life anymore. Now I'm stuck with the remnants of her life before she went into the facility, a storage unit, and no idea what I'm going to do next."

"You're going to celebrate Christmas," Holly said. "You're going to follow your mother's wishes, do what she wants, and celebrate the season you love. Then, we figure it out."

It felt good to be able to really talk to Holly, and it seemed to be bringing us closer. I didn't miss her use of "we" or the rush of emotion it brought me. We needed to talk more. Last night's conversation was a drunken mess, but it was starting to open the floodgates. Now it was time to open them all the way and really be honest with each other.

Chapter Forty-Four

Holly

IT MEANT A LOT TO ME for Lawson to open up the way he had. He'd already shared some of the story with me, and I'd picked up little bits along the way, but this was the first time I felt like he was really just pouring it all out without holding anything back. He shared not only the story of how he ended up visiting Snowflake Hollow and staying at my inn rather than at the house where his family always lived, but also the deep emotions it caused.

Lawson had been a happy, laid-back person from the moment I found myself lying in his arms, looking up into his eyes and wondering if it was possible an angel had scooped me up out of the sky. I believed that was who he really was at his core, but now he was showing me more. There were other layers to him, more depth that only drew me closer to him.

I could see just how much he missed his father and how much he'd admired the man when he was alive. I hadn't had the opportunity to meet his father, but I could imagine he was a pretty incredible man if he was able to capture Gloria's heart the way he had and contribute to raising someone as wonderful as Lawson. I wondered how much of him I was seeing in his son and felt a strange, unexpected sense of gratitude toward the man for the type of man Lawson was.

When he talked about his mother, I could also see his amazing loyalty to her and how committed he was to being a good son. It was touching and encouraging.

But what I was learning about him went beyond just the relationship he had with his parents and how much he appreciated them and admired them for the love they had for each other. When he spoke about how engrossed he got in his company, I could see his intense drive, his intelligence, and just how exceptional he had become.

As soon as that thought went through my mind, I stopped myself. Maybe it wasn't that he had become someone exceptional. That was just who he was. He was exceptional all along. I was only just now finding out.

"I'm sure it was strange for you to have your mother not living in Snowflake Hollow," I said.

Lawson nodded. "This place has always been home. Every time I thought about visiting her, or coming home for a holiday, or anything like that, I always envisioned Snowflake Hollow. Visiting her anywhere else was like she was on vacation and I was just swinging by to say hello. When I found out she was back here, it felt right. Not just for her, but also for me. But I have to admit, it was a little bit odd coming back here after being gone for so long."

"It doesn't really seem all that different than it was when we were in high school," I said.

"Exactly. It's not. That's the point. It isn't different. It's almost the exact same. It just carried right on without me. Not that I thought the whole village was going to come to a screeching halt because I wasn't living here anymore or anything, but it's like I just stepped right back into my space and kept going. I almost felt like the rest of my life hadn't even happened," he said.

"My grandmother never left," I said. "I was the one who jumped ship. And it was really odd leaving Snowflake Hollow. I did it so suddenly. It wasn't like I had a big plan or there was a whole life waiting for me on the outside."

"There wasn't?" Lawson asked. "I always just assumed you'd planned out a bunch of different colleges and had everything set out for you. You were smart, even if your choice of companionship didn't show it."

He flashed me a teasing grin, and I stuck the tip of my tongue out at him in a stunningly mature display of my reaction toward his comment.

"No. I didn't. You can add it to my list of ridiculous failures and stupid decisions, but I actually didn't have anything planned out for after high school. I wanted to go to college, and I'd thought of a few career paths, but I was just so wildly invested in my boyfriend. It's humiliating to even say that now, but I couldn't imagine doing anything without him. I just assumed I would go to the same school as he was going to.

"We would go to classes together and study together. He'd have his football scholarship and be the star, and I'd watch him and be so proud. Then eventually we'd graduate and then get married and the rest of life would happen." I scoffed, shaking my head in disgust at my former self. "Can you believe I was that stupid?"

"You weren't stupid," Lawson said. "That's the last thing I would call you. You were devoted to him. I might not be able to understand it because of who we're talking about, but no one can doubt you dedicated yourself to him and to that relationship."

He started to continue on talking about it, but I shook my head. "I don't really want to talk about him anymore. That's not exactly my favorite aspect of my past."

"Thank goodness, neither do I," Lawson said. "I just thought you were in need of a cleansing moment."

I laughed and shook my head. "Not when it comes to him. I've been over him for a long time. What I'm not over is how much of my life I gave up for and because of him. I left Snowflake Hollow on little more than a whim and just tried to find where life was going to take me. I ended up going to school and building a life for myself, but it's not like it was the life I'd acted out with my Barbies when I was a little girl.

"My grandmother always encouraged me to come back, but she didn't push. She knew I wasn't the biggest fan of this place and wanted me to have my own life. She would come visit me wherever I was, and we kept right up with each other. I had no idea there was anything going on in her life I didn't know about. That goes for the sickness that took her, and for the bed-and-breakfast I'd never even heard about."

"Maybe that was part of it," he said. "She didn't want to tell you about it because she didn't want you to feel obligated to come back here. She knew you had your own life and wanted you to be able to live it."

"I know," I said. "But it makes me wish I knew her better. That I knew more about her. Because it can't just be the bed-and-breakfast. That's not something that just pops up out of nowhere. There had to be more to her wanting to open this place than I knew. Which is why I decided to start it for her."

We were finished eating, and we got up to bring our dishes into the kitchen. The french toast Lawson made was absolutely delicious and the perfect start to another cold December morning. I was definitely going to have to get the recipe from him so I could make them. That made my heart squeeze. I was going to have to be the one making them because he wasn't going to be here.

The conversation we'd had the night before was still in the back of my mind. I wasn't entirely positive everything was clear in my mind because the words had to swim to me through a sea of eggnog, but I knew he told me about his company and the incredible success he already had. I also knew he'd finally confessed his feelings to me and reassured me he wasn't just playing games with me.

But he hadn't made any commitments or promises to stay. I still had to think about him leaving.

"I don't think your grandmother was living some sort of second life," Lawson said. "She was probably the same exact person you knew, she just had this extra part she didn't share with you because she didn't think you could relate."

"Well, she was right about that. The hospitality industry is not something I would have ever chosen to go into if this hadn't shown up in my path. I don't think I'm particularly good at it," I said.

He shook his head at my confession. "I think you underestimate yourself, Holly. You care more about your guests than you let on. And, dare I say it, I think you've been enjoying these yuletide activities. It's in you. It keeps coming out in little bitty sparks, but it's there. Snowflake Hollow got some of its shimmer on you whether you realize it or not."

I smiled as we washed the breakfast dishes. "You know, when I was on the outside, I found myself looking for little things that would remind me of Snowflake Hollow."

He laughed. "You talk about it like it's a prison."

"Not a prison," I said. "But definitely a bubble. It's like we're living in a snow globe. Haven't you ever looked into a snow globe and wondered what life was like for the tiny people living in the little house or who made the teeny snowman?"

"I can't say I ever have," Lawson said.

I thought that was probably a lie, but I was going to go with it. I threw my arms out to the side. "That's because you never had to. You are living in a snow globe."

He laughed. "I think there would need to be a lot more spontaneous snowstorms in order for that to be accurate."

"Even so, there's absolutely a vibe to this place. It feels like it's a different world in a way."

"Is that so bad?" Lawson asked.

"I used to think so," I admitted. "And when I came back after my grandmother died, I really felt like it. But I still didn't have a relationship worth anything, I'd lost my job, I was just kind of treading water and getting really close to sinking. It seemed like there were far worse things out there than hiding out in a bubble for a little while."

"And now?" he asked.

"What do you mean?"

"You said you used to think it was so bad. What about now?"

"I'm still getting used to it, which sounds crazy since I grew up here, but I feel like I'm starting to look at it differently. I'm realizing I like feeling separate from the rest of the world. Here I feel like I'm part of something," I said.

He nodded. "Even the Grinch was a part of Who-Ville."

I splashed him with the bubbly dishwater, and he protested but laughed. I smiled at him, and he kissed me. Not a passionate, hungry kiss—one that was soft and familiar. It felt like the desire and spark between us was really turning into something more.

When we were done with the dishes, we went back out into the front of the house. We were just in time to overhear the conversation between Vint and the rest of his family. His mother tugged his hat down over his head and wrapped his scarf around his neck.

"It's cold out there," she said.

"Just cold," he said with a pout.

"What do you mean?" his mother asked.

"I thought someplace with a name like Snowflake Hollow would have snow for Christmas," he said.

There was a hint of sadness in his voice, and it tugged at my heart. His mother got a briefly sad expression across her face too. She pulled mittens over his hands and gave him the kind of smile mothers do when they are trying to be brave for their children and hate when they are hurt.

"I know, buddy. But it's not like they can make the snow fall. We just have to wait for Mother Nature, and she has decided it isn't time yet. Christmas has still been plenty of fun without snow, and it still will be."

He nodded, and they walked out of the house. Lawson and I looked at each other.

"It sounds like he's dreaming of a White Christmas," he said.

I shook my head at him but a second later perked up. "White Christmas Inn, where you don't have to dream of a White Christmas, because I'm always here."

Now it was Lawson's turn to shake his head. He threw in an uncomfortable wince for good measure.

"I'll keep working on it," I said.

"Alright, we've got to get going," he said, making his way toward my office.

"Get going? Why?"

"You heard him. We have to make some snow."

Chapter Forty-Five

Lawson

"WHAT DO YOU MEAN WE have to make some snow?" Holly asked, eventually falling into step behind me when the apparent shock wore off. "I heard him, but you must have heard his mother. We can't just make snow fall. I know you are good at Christmas and everything, but you can't possibly be that good."

"I might not be able to create actual snow," I said, "but we can make the next best thing."

"Sno-cones?" she asked.

I laughed. "Not exactly. I was thinking more along the lines of fake snow the guests can play with. Mostly Vint, obviously, but I think the older children and even the adults would like it too. We just have to find the right recipe."

I got to her office and stepped aside to wait for her to unlock the door and go in first.

"I would have no idea how to make something like that," she said. "I don't think I've ever even heard of fake snow for people to play with. Unless you're talking about that stuff that puffs out of the machines during parades and at theme parks. But isn't that just soap bubbles? I guess I could fluff up a whole bunch of dish liquid if you think they would like it."

"That wasn't exactly what I was thinking," I said. "But you might be onto something for a summertime activity."

I sat down in the chair behind her desk and wiggled the mouse to wake up her computer screen. The desktop popped right up, and I gave her an incredulous look.

"You don't have a passcode to access your computer?" I asked.

"I keep my office door locked," Holly said. "And I've never had someone storm my office in search of the internet before. Besides, I don't know how many people would actually be interested in being able to access my computer. It's not like there's anything particularly interesting on it."

"Like people's payment information or your banking details?" I asked.

Her face fell a little. "Shit." She cocked her hip and gestured at the computer. "Well, this is why you own your own successful business, and I got myself fired and ended up..."

"Owning your own successful business?"

"Jury is still out on that," she said.

"Which is why we need to keep appealing to the guests as much as possible. We'll talk about your cybersecurity later. For now, we need to find recipes for nontoxic artificial snow."

"Nontoxic is good. I don't need death by chemical exposure showing up on my Yelp reviews," she said, coming up behind me and leaning over to look at the screen.

I looked over my shoulder at her. "I was thinking more along the lines of skin irritation or burning their eyes, but you go right ahead and go there."

I turned back to the screen and brought up a search engine. My search brought up what seemed like endless pages of different recipes and variations for ways to create snow to play in.

"Which one should we use?" Holly asked.

I shrugged. "I've never made any of them, so I'm not sure. I guess we could just pick out a couple of them and try them out. If they don't work, we can always try other ones."

"I like your attitude, Lane," she said. "Be willing to fail upward."

"What does that even mean?" I asked. "I guess there's the whole metaphor of failing as falling down or hitting rock bottom or any of those things. And if you are being successful, you're moving upward or you're moving on up. But if you fail upward, aren't you just succeeding? By merit of upward mobility, you are, in fact, succeeding. Perhaps not at what you originally intended, which can make it seem like a failure, but the end result should be the rubric by which the matter is compared."

Holly stared at me, blinking for a few seconds, and I had a distinct flashback to high school and the many eyes that used to do that exact thing when I spoke to them.

"Well... that... yes," she said. She looked back at the computer. "How about cornstarch and hair conditioner?"

I bit back a laugh and nodded. "Sure. Though, we might want to go to the store and get more conditioner. Fake snow that smells like coconut probably wouldn't get them into the holiday spirit."

A smile curved her lips up as she realized I was talking about the way her hair smelled.

"We can do that. We'll also get some shaving cream. And baking soda and glue."

"Sounds like the forecast is calling for a strange and gooey blizzard," I said.

"Strap on your snowshoes, and let's get this done."

We left her office and bundled up against the sharp cold outside before heading to the car.

"Where do you want to go?" I asked.

It wouldn't have surprised me if she declared herself done with the little stores in town and wanted to head over to the next to go to the big-box store. Instead, she did surprise me with her answer.

"Mary and Brighton's," she said. "They'll have everything we need."

I gave a single nod. "Alright. Here we go."

With the days before Christmas dwindling down, the crowd inside the general store had ticked up quite a bit since the last time we were there. People searching out the perfect gift for their neighbor or coworker, finding things to stuff into stockings, or even just joining in on the fun of the last-minute hustle made the aisles tight, and Holly pressed close against my back rather than standing at my side to make it easier to navigate.

We went to the hair care aisle first and grabbed several bottles of every white conditioner we could find that didn't have a strong fruity smell. I even found one that had a mint scent, which seemed like the perfect match. Next, we scooped up most of the shelf of shaving cream and then headed for the baking aisle. The shelf that was supposed to be holding baking soda was empty, but I gestured over to Brighton and asked if they had any in the back room.

"I'll go check. I think we just got a shipment," he said.

"Perfect. Thank you."

"I'll be right back," Holly said. "I need to look at something."

I nodded, and she disappeared into the crowd. Several minutes later, she and Brighton came back toward me from opposite directions. She wasn't holding anything, so I assumed she hadn't found what she was looking for. Brighton, on the other hand, had a pallet of baking soda and a grin on his face. Holly and I thanked him and gathered up several pounds. We didn't know exactly what we were doing, but we were prepared for whatever it was that happened.

"Is this what it's supposed to look like?" Holly asked when our first batch was finished and she was poking at the somewhat gelatinous mass in the bowl.

I was glad we thought to pick up several new cheap mixing bowls for the experiment. I had a feeling some of this might not turn out great, and

I didn't want to ruin the mixing bowls she used on a regular basis with hardened faux snow.

"I'm not sure," I said. "I'm not exactly an authority on fake snow. But something isn't feeling quite right."

"I've definitely never played in snow like this," she said.

"Ah," I said. "Now we're getting down to the truth. Holly the Humbug plays in snow."

"Did you just call me Holly the Humbug?" she asked.

I gestured across my chest. "I'm thinking of getting it put on a shirt for you."

She thought about it for a second, then gave a half shrug. "Can't say no to branding." She let out a sigh and looked down at the bowl again. "I think we did something wrong. Let's try a different recipe."

Over the next hour, we laughed our way through each of the recipes we'd picked out, and while we had some successes, things got progressively messier. We'd just filled the largest bowl with another good batch when I noticed Holly had streaks of fake snow in her hair and along her face, and her clothes were splotched and spattered in the various ingredients.

I couldn't help myself. I pulled her toward me, and we kissed passionately. As she pulled her lips away from mine, I held her tight, and she giggled. I leaned down so I could whisper into her ear, and as my lips brushed the bottom lobe, the smell of her perfume filled my senses.

"I think we should get you all cleaned up. How does a hot shower sound?" I asked.

I pulled back to look into her eyes and saw the excitement build there. She nodded, biting down on her bottom lip, and then pulled away, holding one hand out for me to take as I followed her out and to the stairs. I looked back at the mess we made and shook my head.

We'd clean that up later.

We went to her room, and I closed the door behind us. Holly was already walking ahead, on her way to her bathroom, her shirt above her head. She tossed it away to the clothes bin and kept walking, not looking back. Next, her thumbs were in her pants and pushing them down. My stomach clenched as the sight of the red thong, representing the last thing she was wearing, disappeared as she closed the bathroom door.

I hurried to take off my clothes, leaving them piled by the basket, and turned the knob of the bathroom door. The shower was already on, and the lacy red thong was on the floor. My cock was hard and standing at attention as I grabbed the shower curtain and peeled it back.

Holly stood under the water, leaning back as she wet her hair. Thick, round droplets of water cascaded down her tight, curvy body. I stepped in, and she opened her eyes, a devious grin on her face. She pulled me toward her, and the water covered me, warming me up and relaxing the muscles on my neck.

Holly pressed a kiss to my chest as I wiped water away from my eyes. She knelt in front of me, kissing my chest, my stomach, my hips. I watched her as she let her tongue slide out and brush across the side of my cock, her eyes flickering up to mine. She wanted to see me react. I had no intention of disappointing her.

She took me into her lips, and I groaned softly. The warmth of her tongue as she rolled it around the head of my cock was nearly enough to make me come right then, but I held on. She plunged down, taking me deep in her throat, one hand sliding underneath to massage my balls. I let one hand fill with her wet hair and guided her in deep, slow strokes as she sucked me.

Her hand wrapped around the base of my member and stroked and a deep, needful moan bubbled up from her throat. There was no use in holding back. She didn't want me to anyway. I closed my eyes and let my head fall back into the stream of water as I came, and she took me in her mouth. But I wasn't done yet. Not by a long shot.

Chapter Forty-Six

Holly

LAWSON PULLED ME UP and I pressed kisses to his chest as he did. He pushed me against the wall and pressed his own kisses to my neck and began to work his way down. One hand slid down my body and between my thighs, and I groaned delightedly at the powerful way his hands moved, so confidently to my core.

He took one nipple into his mouth and rolled his tongue around it, and I closed my eyes to focus on his touch. A thick, knowledgeable finger was resting at my entrance, and I gasped as it slipped inside. Using his thumb to brush through my folds, he penetrated me deeper, and I felt my body tense as the sensation overwhelmed me.

Letting my nipple free from his lips, he kissed down my stomach, tasting me and licking up the streams of hot water as they tumbled down from above. I reached up and turned the showerhead so that it mostly hit him on his back as he knelt down and pulled one leg up and over his shoulder so it didn't drown him.

His tongue flickered out and brushed across the sides of my lower lips, and I moaned. His finger was deep inside me, gently rubbing against my upper wall, and I felt myself nearing what would undoubtedly be the first of several climaxes. As he licked through my folds, his other hand reached behind me and held me still, showing me the power of his control and the determination to please me at the same time. It was intoxicating.

I let my head rest against the wall of the shower as he licked me, the tip of his tongue creating magic between my thighs. I felt the explosiveness of an intense orgasm coming, and I filled my hands with his hair. The moans were getting shorter, more rapid now, and I felt my body hitching, the oxygen leaving my head as I gave in to the sensations that were building.

Lawson's finger pressed against the top wall and his tongue into my clit as I buckled in his grip. He held me up as I shook and rocked my hips, the wave of an intense climax washing over me. He lapped it up below me, just as I had done for him, moaning with his own pleasure at feeling me come. I looked down, my jaw locked open as I vibrated, and my hands reached for the wall to hold me up. The finger that had been inside me slipped out, and I watched as he used that hand to stroke himself. He was still hard.

He made his way back up my body, and our lips met as he stood. Our tongues wrestled with each other as I wrapped my arms around him, and my body tingled at the thought of what came next. He was still stroking himself, slowly and deliberately, and his eyes locked onto mine as he pulled away from me. He was pleasuring himself to the sight of my body, and it made me feel incredibly sexy and alive. I stepped back to watch him, to let my eyes roam over his body as the water cascaded over tensed muscles and the thickness of his cock as he slid it between his palm and fingers.

I reached behind me and grabbed the bottle of bodywash and filled my palm with it. Holding my hands in the water, I let it lather up and then pressed it onto my body. His eyes narrowed in concentration as he stroked himself faster while I covered myself in the fragrant bubbles. Then I stepped closer to him and pressed my body into his, rubbing myself on him and covering him with the soap as well.

We kissed under the stream of water that slowly cleaned us, and my body was slippery and slick. His hand ran over my chest and filled with my breast, squeezing it as he moaned. I reached behind him as the water washed the rest of the water away and turned off the faucet. As the water stopped, his eyes opened, and his lips spread in a grin.

I stepped out of the shower, grabbing a towel and brushing it across my body as I made my way to the bed. I didn't care if the sheets got a little wet. I was going to have to change them anyway.

I crawled onto the bed, but before I could get too far, Lawson's hand wrapped around my ankle and stopped me. I was on all fours, and I froze, looking back with a grin. Lawson climbed onto the bed behind me and ran his hands over my ass, using his thumbs to pull the skin up as he reached for my hips. I settled on my knees and arched my back as he positioned himself. My pussy tingled and throbbed in anticipation.

Lawson rested the head of his cock at my entrance and slowly pushed it inside. I was soaking wet and ready for him, and he slid in deeply, easily, and then stretched me as he pushed all the way in. The tightness inside me gave way to intense pleasure as I cried out into the pillow below me. Achingly slowly, he pulled his cock nearly all the way out of me and then plunged back in again, filling me and sending my body into the throes of a pre-climax.

"Fuck me, please," I moaned, my voice muffled by the pillow.

Lawson's hands clenched tight over my hips, and he began to thrust, to slam into me with an intensity that shattered my thin grip on reality. I toppled over into revolving orgasms as he dominated me, his body so perfectly molded to give mine the most intense pleasure, and as we rolled around in the bed, changing positions, I reached a nirvana that made me feel like our souls touched, tangled, and exploded in a euphoria of orgasmic pleasure.

When he came, I came with him, and we fell into the bed, giggling and cooing at each other until his body stopped clenching and the last of his essence was emptied inside me.

I would have liked to just stay right there in Lawson's arms for the rest of the afternoon and evening, but being warm and cozy with him wasn't a good enough excuse to ignore the guests. They didn't know about the snow surprise, but the mess downstairs was going to give them a hint when they made their way back to the bed-and-breakfast.

I would rather them come back to something fun than to think I'd gone mad during one of my baking experiments and was now lying in wait somewhere. With one more kiss, I reluctantly got out of bed and pulled fresh clothes out of the dresser. Lawson got up and wrapped the sheet from my bed around himself.

"My clothes are covered in fake snow, so I think I'm just going to go like this," he said.

I laughed. "Emperor of the snowfall?"

"I like it," he said. "I don't think any of the guests are here right now, so I'm just going to make a run for it. I'll meet you back downstairs to help you clean up and get the play area ready."

"Where do you think we should set it up?"

We looked at each other.

"Outside," we said at the same moment.

I was about to point out how cold it was, then realized we were talking about creating a snow experience, and people were generally accustomed to the feeling of cold when it came to playing in the snow.

"Alright. Here I go. If you hear Nancy screaming, it means I got caught."

I giggled. "Okay."

Lawson took a breath. "Alright. Here I go."

Throwing the door to the bedroom open, he ran out into the house. I laughed as I listened to his heavy footsteps thudding down the hall and then in the distance going up the stairs. I finished getting dressed, dried my hair, and threw on some makeup so I would look put together when everybody got back. Gathering up the dirty clothes, I brought them to the laundry room and got a load going before heading into the kitchen to put together the afternoon snack.

The guests were rarely around in the afternoons as we got closer to Christmas, but I dreaded the moment when I didn't have something ready to offer them and they all swarmed in ravenous from their day of merriment. So, I made sure there was at least something simple sitting out for a while in the afternoons. That day it was the old standby cheese and crackers. Maybe not innovative and interesting, but it did the trick, and I could chalk it up to tradition.

Cleaning up the snow mess wasn't as difficult as I thought, and soon we were outside smoothing a tarp across the grass so we could fill it up with snow for the guests to play in. It didn't look like enough, so while Lawson went to find something to create a barrier around the edge of the tarp, I went back inside to concoct a few more batches. We might have nearly bought Mary and Brighton's out of baking soda, cornstarch, and shaving cream, but it was all going to a good cause.

When I came back out laden with bowls of snow, Lawson was piling up inflatable pool toys around the edge of the snow area.

"Where did you find those?" I asked.

"In the shed. It looks like they've never been used."

"Well, there's no pool," I said.

"Maybe an idea for expansion," he said with a wink.

I brought the snow over to him, and he nodded his approval. Stepping back, he surveyed the inflatables, then reached for one of a stack of old sheets.

"Those are just sheets from my grandmother's house," I said. "I put them out there because I thought they could be used for something."

"And now they are," Lawson said. He shook out one of the sheets and let it drape over the toys. "Instant snowbank."

At the street, a truck pulled up, and one of the young clerks from Mary and Brighton's jumped out of the driver's side. He ran around to the back of the truck and dropped the tailgate so he could tug a large cardboard box out.

I smiled and started down toward the clerk.

"I'm sorry the delivery took so long," he said. "We're really busy."

"Not a problem," I said. "Thank you for getting it to me. Can you just bring it up a bit closer to the house?"

"Sure thing."

I followed him across the lawn and indicated where to drop it, then reached in my pocket and pulled out a tip for him.

"Thank you," I said.

"Merry Christmas," he said and scurried back to the truck.

"What's that?" Lawson asked, coming over after finishing draping the toys.

I started tearing away at the thick layers of tape holding the box closed. The clerk had put it down on the grass so the picture on the front was concealed, but when I finally managed to wrestle the box open, it revealed the folded-up mound of vinyl and a small compressor.

"I got my own inflatable."

Ten minutes later, a cheerful snowman towered over the lawn, the sound of the compressor keeping him filled with air almost like a wintery wind if you put a lot of imagination into it. I'd finally broken down. I was one of those lawns now.

Chapter Forty-Seven

Lawson

"WELL, THIS WAS UNEXPECTED," I said.

"Why would you say that?" she asked cheekily, looking up at her snowman with a shocking amount of pride.

"I don't know, something about not getting into the spirit of Christmas and all that," I said. "And now I'm staring at what has to be a ten-foot snowman in your lawn."

"Yeah, yeah," she said. "He's cute. Like, even aside from Christmas time, he's just cute."

"And big. Very large."

"Yes, well, the other option was a twenty-five foot one and I thought that might be a bit much," she laughed.

"You think?" I joked. "No, I admire your ambition. And your restraint, apparently. It was just unexpected."

"I am nothing if not a wealth of surprises," she said.

I pulled her tight to me and pressed a kiss to her lips.

"Yes, you are," I said. "So, what else are we going to do?"

"I don't know," she said. "I was thinking some kind of wintery treat. It's not like they can eat snowballs."

"Well, not these," I said. "But we could make snowballs that are edible."

"What, you mean like those things at the gas station?"

"Yeah," I said. "The ones with the marshmallow inside. They shouldn't be too hard to make, and you probably already have the ingredients here."

"Good, because I have no intention of going to the store again," she laughed. "I just want to be here."

"Me too," I said. "Though I'd go out if you needed me to."

"No." She grinned. "I need you here. With me."

"Deal," I said, leaning in for another kiss. "Alright, so we make snowball cakes. We just have to rummage through the pantries and see if we have the stuff to make them first. Maybe meringues?"

"Meringues?" she asked. "Do we need to go over my baking reputation again?"

"You did great with the cookies, remember?"

"It's a far cry to go from making some cookies with help to making batches of meringues—which, by the way, I haven't the faintest idea how to do—and snowball cakes," she said.

"Ah, come on," I said, "you'll be fine. The cookies went great, and that should tell you, you have it in you. Come on, this will be fun."

"Alright," she agreed reluctantly. "Let's head to the pantry first."

We dipped inside, going straight to the pantry door and opening it up. It was one of the old-style pantries, where a person could walk in and the shelves went from almost the floor up to nearly the ceiling. There were tons of soups and canned vegetables there, but the collection of baking goods was rather slim. It was clearly a pantry she had stocked before I arrived and had done so with the knowledge and assurance that the oven was going to be primarily for baking lasagnas and pizza.

"Not a whole lot of baking stuff here," I said. "However, there is this."

I held up a bag over oversized marshmallows.

"Hey, my s'more kit marshmallows," she said excitedly. "I had been looking for those."

"They were behind a family-sized can of tomato soup that I can only guess is intended for a family of twelve," I said. "Here, take that. Those will be perfect for the snowballs." I noticed another two bags behind the one I had pulled out. "You have three bags of marshmallows for s'mores?"

"I like s'mores," she said sheepishly. "So what?"

"Nothing." I shook my head. "You're just adorable."

"Here's the cocoa powder. And coconut shreds."

"Awesome," I said, gathering the rest of the ingredients needed for the cakes. "Now we just need to find some cream of tartar and we are good to go."

"For the meringues?" she asked.

"Hey, now you're getting it," I laughed.

"It isn't that I don't understand what goes in the things that I failed to bake correctly," she said. "I just seem to blank out around the time I put them in the oven."

Laughing, I gathered the rest of the ingredients needed and brought them over in a giant mixing bowl to the kitchen table. Setting them all out, I made a little station for mixing and set out a couple of mixing bowls and measuring spoons and cups.

"Meringue's first," I said. "Can you preheat the oven to two-twenty-five?"

"Sure," she said, crossing the kitchen and punching the number into the oven.

"I have an idea to make these Christmas-appropriate," I said. "Where are the rest of those peppermint sticks?"

"The ones I put out for the guests in the living room?"

"The ones that look like little peppermint cigars and are sugary?" I asked.

"Yes," she said.

"Those, yes."

"I have a couple other boxes of them in the bottom of the China cabinet," she said.

She ran off to grab them while I began separating out egg whites. When she returned, she sat six boxes of the peppermints on the table, and I began beating the whites, tartar, and salt into soft peaks.

"Good, now put a few of them into a zip-top bag," I said. She did as I asked, and as the peaks began to form, she laid the bag on the table. "Now, crush the peppermints."

"With what?" she asked.

"A pan? A pot? A hammer?"

"Yeah, like I just have hammers lying around," she said.

"Second drawer from the wall on the right," I said. "It's your junk drawer."

"I was not aware I had a junk drawer," she said, her lips pursing up on one side.

I shrugged.

"You do now," I said. "A pan will do, though."

She grabbed a pan from the dish drainer and sat it over the bag of peppermints and then pressed down in the center, crushing them. When they were all crushed up and I had added sugar until the peaks were stiff, I pulled out the prepared cookie sheets. Putting a clump on the sheets about an inch apart, I then looked over at Holly and motioned to the peppermints.

"Now?" she asked.

I nodded.

Holly sprinkled bits of crushed peppermint over the meringues and then sat back satisfied as I dipped the oven. Closing the door, I set a timer for ninety minutes and turned around to face her.

"Now we wait," I said. "While we do that, we should make the snow-balls."

As we made the little treats, the meringues cooked, and I turned on some Christmas music to listen to. It was fun, and I could see the ap-prehension and distance from allowing herself to enjoy the season slipping away from her. She was starting to get into it. Holly was becoming a Christmas person in front of my eyes.

"You know," I said as we cleaned up the creation station we had made and I cracked open the oven to let the meringues cool in place for a while, "there is one other thing we should have that I am pretty sure you are out of."

"What's that?" she asked.

"Whipped cream," I said.

"Crap. I should have gotten more of it at the store."

"Well, yes, but, we could always make some fresh whipped cream."

Slowly, her face softened and became wistful. The corners of her eyes became wet and glossed over as she held back a sudden tear. I walked over to her and held her by the elbows, searching her face.

"Hey, what's going on?" I asked.

"It's nothing," she said. "Just a sudden and very visceral memory of my grandmother."

"Tell me," I said, offering a smile.

"When I was little—like really little," she said, "my favorite thing in the world was to sit on the couch with a big bowl of whipped cream my grandmother would make. She would sprinkle them with chocolate chips and call it Dalmatian cream."

"That's so cute," I said.

"Yeah," she laughed, wiping away a tear. "Ever since, I will sit down with a big bowl and a can and just go to town sometimes." She shook her head. "It's probably not the healthiest dessert, but it's delicious."

"Classy," I said. "It's a super-classy dessert for a super-classy lady. Just shows off your pedigree."

She laughed, smacking me playfully on the arm.

"Homemade would be great," she said.

"Do you know how to make it?" I asked. "I think I do, but we might have to look it up."

"All I remember is she used to stick a bowl in the freezer first," she said. "Oh, wait. Cream, powdered sugar, and vanilla!"

"You remember? Have you made it?"

"Not since I was a little kid," she said.

We stuck a bowl in the freezer and tended to the snowballs, finishing those up while the glass bowl got cold. When we brought it out, she took over, making the whipped cream from memories long dormant in her mind. I watched her, fascinated, and when it was mostly done, I stuck a finger in it to taste.

"Delicious," I said. "Though technically, this is Chantilly cream."

She stared at me, one eyebrow raised.

"See, this is why you wouldn't have known me in high school much. I was a nerd."

"No," she said, shaking her head and smiling. "I would have found you fascinating then just like I do now. I wish I had the chance back then."

"Well, you have the chance now," I said.

"Yeah," she said, nodding and smiling wide. "I sure do."

Chapter Forty-Eight

Holly

LAWSON AND I WENT INTO the storage room in the house and brought out a couple of banquet tables to set up on the front porch. We draped them in white tablecloths and set out all the snow-themed treats we'd made along with the Crock-Pot of hot cocoa and all the toppings.

"Are you sure they are even going to want more cocoa?" I asked, second-guessing the plan, and I crawled around trying to find the outdoor electrical outlet so I could plug in the pot to keep the cocoa warm. "It seems like we've given it to them with all the special add-ins and everything a lot over the last couple of weeks."

"Not all of these guests were here for those," Lawson said. "And even if they were, it's Christmas. That means hot cocoa. It's not like it's a limited-edition beverage. People drink cocoa all through the winter."

We'd just gone back inside for all the serving utensils and come out to arrange it all when Vint's family and another set of guests pulled into the parking area one right after the other. They parked, and I drew in a breath. It was the moment of truth.

I didn't know why I felt so nervous waiting for them to come into the yard and discover the surprise. It wasn't like the cookies or the eggnog or the singalong when they had expectations about it. And yet, somehow, that made me more anxious. It was as if those expectations meant they'd given me guidelines. They knew what they wanted, and it was just up to me to take that information and actually make it happen. If I didn't do it well, at least it was just that I'd failed in that particular way.

With this, I felt strangely vulnerable. It wasn't a classic Christmas tradition. It wasn't something they'd asked for. I couldn't rely totally on Lawson to give me insight into what they wanted so I could try to make it happen. This was something he and I came up with to give them a surprise, and part of me worried they would think it was ridiculous.

Lawson and I walked down the steps and waited at the bottom for them. The families were chatting among themselves as they walked along the narrow path from the parking area to the front of the house and at first it seemed like they hadn't even noticed the giant snowman. I found that difficult to believe considering they would have had to have seen it while driving up toward the house.

Suddenly, Vint broke through his parents and rushed forward. He stopped a few feet in front of them and stared up at the snowman, drawing in a long, awe-filled breath.

"It's amazing," he said. He looked over his shoulder at his parents. "Look! Look at the snowman."

"It's a good snowman," his father said, coming up to wrap his arm around his son's shoulders.

"Maybe it will bring real snow," the little boy said.

"I wouldn't get your hopes up too much," his mother said. "He's very cute, but I don't know if he can change the weather."

"He might," Vint said. "He could be a magic snowman."

"Well, I don't know how well his magic is working yet this season because he's brand-new, but we do have something close to snow for you," Lawson said. He gestured toward the snow play area we set up. "You can go play in it." He looked at the little boy's parents. "If it's okay with your parents, of course."

He looked up at them with bright, hopeful eyes, and they nodded. The instant he got their approval, he ran forward and jumped over the inflatable snowbank onto the tarp. His foot hit the slippery surface, and he immediately fell down hard. I clutched Lawson's shirt, waiting for the inevitable scream. This was just perfect. I tried to make holiday magic, and I broke a child.

But there was no scream. Instead, he let out a delighted laugh and reached forward to fill his hands with the fake snow. Everybody let out a sigh of relief, and I noticed another of the families had appeared behind them. The teenage girl who had spent so much of her visit sitting sullenly and wondering when anything was going to happen was peering around her father standing in front of her, looking at the snow. There was a hint of something in her eyes, like she was remembering what it was like to be a child.

"I'm sure he would like someone to play with," I said. The girl looked up at me like she'd been caught, and I nodded toward the snow and the giggling little boy. "Go ahead. It's just fake snow." I lowered my voice and leaned toward her a little. "You can even call it a science experiment."

A grin broke across her face, and she ran for the snow. Vint offered her a handful of the mush, and she took it happily, molding it and squishing it between her hands. Slowly, the other guests made their way across the grass, and soon nearly all of them had handfuls of the fake snow. The pool inflatables didn't stand up to the expectation of being a barrier and were soon shed of their sheets and deconstructed from their snowbank piles, but it didn't matter. Even with some being used as seats and some scattered on the grass, it looked perfect.

As they played, Lawson and I brought their attention over to the treats on the porch. A couple of the adults came up and perused the offerings, filling up napkins and snowflake-decorated paper plates to bring back down to the snow area to share with their families. And just like Lawson said, the hot cocoa was a big hit.

When we were first planning the play area for the guests, I assumed we would just set it up and then I'd leave them to their own devices, but it didn't work out that way. I ended up standing out on the porch watching them, going in and out of the kitchen to replenish the cocoa and other treats, and even getting in on the playing myself a bit.

The guests were obviously having a blast, and it felt really good to see that. There was a genuine sense of joy in them, something that just came from having fun and making memories together. These were people who didn't know each other until they came to the bed-and-breakfast, and yet they weren't just sticking to their families and only interacting with them. They were talking, laughing, and playing together. Something about the thought of these families showing up in the vacation pictures constantly being snapped on phones throughout the group made my heart warm.

As I was filling the plate of snowball cakes back up, Lawson came over and rested his hand on my lower back.

"I'll be right back," he said and kissed my cheek before rushing off.

I was worried as I watched him leave. He hadn't said where he was going and seemed to be in a rush. I hoped his mother or the facility hadn't called with something wrong. But I tried not to show my worry and kept having fun with the guests. They stayed out playing even as the sun started going down, stopping only when the temperature had dropped considerably and all of them were getting tired.

They thanked me for the surprise, and I noticed Vint run over and hug the inflatable snowman as his parents tried to herd him inside. He whispered something to the inflatable before bounding up onto the porch.

"That was great," he said.

He was covered head to toe in the foamy mixture, and I was sure the washer was going to be getting a workout the next day, but I wasn't too worried about it. Baking soda and body care products were by far not the worst things that the machine had dealt with, I was sure.

Lawson still wasn't back, but I went to work cleaning up by the glow of the snowman's internal lights and the porch light. I brought the dishes into the kitchen, and when I came out, Lawson was walking through the yard.

"Be right back," he said again and went inside.

This time, he actually came back moments later. He helped me get the last of the dishes inside and pack away the few leftover treats, then stripped off the tablecloths and brought them to the laundry. We folded the tables and put them back in storage, then stepped out and looked out over the yard. It was covered in fake snow and pool floats, a couple of pieces of dropped treats, and a balled-up tarp.

"I'll start deflating the toys," I said with a sigh.

He laughed. "Just open them up and bring them up to put under the porch so the wind doesn't take them away. Tomorrow we'll drag them back out and take a hose to them all and the grass."

"Sounds good to me."

We finished getting everything put away and went inside to clean up. I came downstairs and went into the kitchen to pour drinks for our usual evening together on the porch, thinking he might tell me what was going on then. Lawson was already in the kitchen, and when I walked up to the counter, I noticed he had a big glass bowl in front of him and was filling it with a mound of freshly made whipped cream.

"What's that for?" I asked.

He opened up a cabinet and pulled out a bag from the candy shop. Grinning, he reached in and pulled out a cellophane sack of Christmas-colored chocolate chips.

"It took forever for me to get them," he said. "The line was all the way out the door and down the sidewalk. Most of their stock was gone. I bought all the chocolate chips they had left."

He opened up the bag and sprinkled the chips over the whipped cream, then reached in the drawer for two spoons.

"You did that for me?" I asked.

"Of course," he said. "You are doing so much to make sure everyone else gets their traditions and happy memories. You can go without your own."

An unexpected surge of nostalgia and emotion came over me, and I kissed him.

"Thank you."

"You're welcome."

We gathered up blankets and our drinks and carried them along with the whipped cream and chocolate chips out onto the porch. Cuddling up together on the porch swing, we each took a bite of the simple but meaningful treat. Lawson made an approving sound.

"See?" I said. "It's delicious."

I leaned my head over to rest on his shoulder and let out a sigh. He kissed the top of my head and rested his on it. I was settling into deep relaxation when his head suddenly popped up and his body went tense.

"Holly, look," he said.

"What? What is it?"

"Look at the snowman," he said.

At first, I worried it had broken free of its stakes and was starting to drift away. I didn't want to try to tackle a ten-foot-tall inflatable snowman in the dark. But then I saw what he was pointing out. Not the snowman itself, but in the light coming off it.

Snowflakes.

They were light and delicate, but they were there.

"It's snowing," I said.

Lawson let out a shocked laugh. "It's snowing."

As we watched, the flakes got denser, and soon we could see them falling heavily right beside us. I couldn't believe it. Maybe the snowman was magical after all.

THE END

OF
PART 8

Snowflake
HOLLOW
12 DAYS OF CHRISTMAS
ADVENT CALENDARS
3   12   7   5
10   9   2   4
6   1   8   11
NEW CHAPTER EVERY DAY

Find Lexy Timms:

LEXY TIMMS NEWSLETTER:
   http://www.lexytimms/newsletter
   Lexy Timms Facebook Page:
   https://www.facebook.com/SavingForever
   Lexy Timms Website:
   http://www.lexytimms.com

Lexy
Timms
Managing
BOSSES
BOSS
BOSS
BOSS
Lexy
Timms
FREE
for a
Limited
Time

Want

FREE READS?

Sign up for Lexy Timms' newsletter
And she'll send you updates on new releases,
ARC copies of books and a whole lotta fun!

Sign up for news and updates!
http://www.lexytimms/newsletter

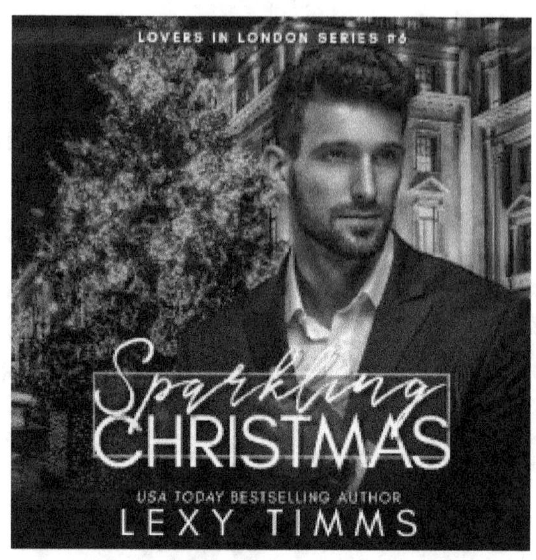

Fake
BILLIONAIRE
SERIES
Fake
CHRISTMAS
USA TODAY BESTSELLING AUTHOR
LEXY TIMMS

BUTLER
FITNESS
SERIES
All
Wrapped
Up
USA TODAY BESTSELLING AUTHOR
LEXY TIMMS

Don't miss out!

Visit the website below and you can sign up to receive emails whenever Lexy Timms publishes a new book. There's no charge and no obligation.

https://books2read.com/r/B-A-NNL-EKVTB

BOOKS 2 READ

Connecting independent readers to independent writers.

Did you love *Snowflake Hollow - Part 8*? Then you should read *Managing the Bosses Box Set #1-3*[1] by Lexy Timms!

<u>Grab Managing the Bosses Box Set Books #1-3</u>
  Book 1 The Boss
  *From USA TODAY Bestselling Author, Lexy Timms, comes a billionaire romance that'll make you swoon and fall in love all over again.*Jamie Connors has given up on finding a man. Despite being smart, pretty, and just slightly overweight, she's a magnet for the kind of guys that don't stay around.Her sister's wedding is at the foreground of the family's attention. Jamie would be fine with it if her sister wasn't pressuring her to lose weight so she'll fit in the maid of honor dress, her mother would get off her case and her ex-boyfriend wasn't about to become her brother-in-law.Determined to step out on her own, she accepts a PA position from

billionaire Alex Reid. The job includes an apartment on his property and gets her out of living in her parent's basement.Jamie has to balance her life and somehow figure out how to manage her billionaire boss, without falling in love with him.

Book 2 The Boss Too

Jamie Connors has decided a job is more important than a boyfriend. She's landed an awesome position working as billionaire Alex Reid's personal PA. It is not meant to be a job with benefits and yet she finds herself in Alex' bed. Despite being smart, pretty, and slightly overweight, she doesn't believe she's attractive enough for a man like Alex.Trying to manage work and put as much time into her sister's wedding, Jamie finds herself trying to please everyone. Her sister's wedding is at the foreground of the family's attention. Jamie would be fine if her sister wasn't so bossy, if her mother would stop nagging and her awful ex-boyfriend wasn't about to become her brother-in-law.Jamie has to learn to love herself again, speak up for herself and have the confidence to go after what she wants. She also needs to prove to Alex that she's perfect for her job and for his bed.

Book 3 Who's the Boss Now

How close can you get to the fire and not get burned? Landing the dream job, working and dating her incredibly hot boss and at the same time gaining the confidence she never had, Jamie doesn't think live could get any better.She's helping to manage a multi-billion dollar company. Her family issues seemed to be resolved and even though she and Alex have to figure out the wrinkles, it looks like they'll be able to be professional at work and romantic after.Except perfect isn't quite exactly how Jamie imagined it would be.

Managing the Bosses Series: The Boss The Boss Too Who's the Boss Now * Gift for the Boss (Christmas Novella) Love the Boss I Do the Boss Wife to the Boss Employed by the Boss Brother to the Boss Senior Advisor to the Boss Forever the Boss

Christmas with the Boss

Billionaire in Control

Billionaire Makes Millions
Billionaire at Work
Mark's Story - Precious Little Thing
Mark's Story - Priceless Love
Valentine Love
The Cost of Freedom
Trick or Treat
The Night Before Christmas
This is a steamy romance, NOT erotica.
Read more at www.lexytimms.com.

Also by Lexy Timms

12 Days of Christmas
Snowflake Hollow - Part 1
Snowflake Hollow - Part 2
Snowflake Hollow - Part 3
Snowflake Hollow - Part 4
Snowflake Hollow - Part 5
Snowflake Hollow - Part 6
Snowflake Hollow - Part 7
Snowflake Hollow - Part 8

A Bad Boy Bullied Romance
I Hate You
I Hate You A Little Bit
I Hate You A Little Bit More

A Bump in the Road Series
Expecting Love
Selfless Act
Doctor's Orders

A Burning Love Series
Spark of Passion
Flame of Desire
Blaze of Ecstasy

A Chance at Forever Series
Forever Perfect
Forever Desired
Forever Together

A Dark Mafia Romance Series
Taken By The Mob Boss
Truce With The Mob Boss
Taking Over the Mob Boss
Trouble For The Mob Boss
Tailored By The Mob Boss
Tricking the Mob Boss

A Dating App Series
I've Been Matched
You've Been Matched
We've Been Matched

A "Kind of" Billionaire

Taking a Risk
Safety in Numbers
Pretend You're Mine

A Maybe Series
Maybe I Should
Maybe I Shouldn't
Maybe I Did

Assisting the Boss Series
Billion Reasons
Duke of Delegation
Late Night Meetings
Delegating Love
Suitors and Admirers

BBW Romance Series
Capturing Her Beauty
Pursuing Her Dreams
Tracing Her Curves

Beating the Biker Series
Making Her His
Making the Break
Making of Them

Betrayal at the Bay Series
Devil's Bay
Devil's Deceit
Devil's Duplicity

Billionaire Banker Series
Banking on Him
Price of Passion
Investing in Love
Knowing Your Worth
Treasured Forever
Banking on Christmas
Billionaire Banker Box Set Books #1-3

Billionaire CEO Brothers
Tempting the Player
Late Night Boardroom
Reviewing the Perfomance
Result of Passion
Directing the Next Move
Touching the Assets

Billionaire Hitman Series
The Hit
The Job
The Run

Billionaire Holiday Romance Series
Driving Home for Christmas
The Valentine Getaway
Cruising Love
Billionaire Holiday Romance Box Set

Billionaire in Disguise Series
Facade
Illusion
Charade

Billionaire Secrets Series
The Secret
Freedom
Courage
Trust
Impulse
Billionaire Secrets Box Set Books #1-3

Blind Sight Series
See Me
Fix Me
Eyes On Me

Counting the Kisses

Cry Wolf Reverse Harem Series
Beautiful & Wild
Misunderstood
Never Tamed

Darkest Night Series
Savage
Vicious
Brutal
Sinful
Fierce

Diamond in the Rough Anthology
Billionaire Rock
Billionaire Rock - part 2

Dirty Little Taboo Series
Flirting Touch
Denying Pleasure
Forbidding Desire
Craving Passion

Dominating PA Series

Her Personal Assistant - Part 1
Her Personal Assistant - Part 2
Her Personal Assistant Box Set

Fake Billionaire Series
Faking It
Temporary CEO
Caught in the Act
Never Tell A Lie
Fake Christmas
Fake Billionaire Box Set #1-3

Firehouse Romance Series
Caught in Flames
Burning With Desire
Craving the Heat
Firehouse Romance Complete Collection

Forging Billions Series
Dirty Money
Petty Cash
Payment Required

For His Pleasure
Elizabeth
Georgia

Madison

Fortune Riders MC Series
Billionaire Biker
Billionaire Ransom
Billionaire Misery
Fortune Riders Box Set - Books #1-3

Fragile Series
Fragile Touch
Fragile Kiss
Fragile Love

Great Temptation Series
The Devil's Footsteps
Heaven's Command
Mortals Surrender

Hades' Spawn Motorcycle Club
One You Can't Forget
One That Got Away
One That Came Back
One You Never Leave
One Christmas Night
Hades' Spawn MC Complete Series

Hard Rocked Series
Rhyme
Harmony
Lyrics

Heart of Stone Series
The Protector
The Guardian
The Warrior

Heart of the Battle Series
Celtic Viking
Celtic Rune
Celtic Mann
Heart of the Battle Series Box Set

Heistdom Series
Master Thief
Goldmine
Diamond Heist
Smile For Me
Your Move
Green With Envy
Saving Money

Highlander Wolf Series
Pack Run
Pack Land
Pack Rules

Hollyweird Fae Series
Inception of Gold
Disruption of Magic
Guardians of Twilight

How To Love A Spy
The Secret
The Secret Life
The Secret Wife

Just About Series
About Love
About Truth
About Forever
Just About Box Set Books #1-3

Justice Series
Seeking Justice
Finding Justice

Chasing Justice
Pursuing Justice
Justice - Complete Series

Karma Series
Walk Away
Make Him Pay
Perfect Revenge

Kissed by Billions
Kissed by Passion
Kissed by Desire
Kissed by Love

Leaning Towards Trouble
Trouble
Discord
Tenacity

Love on the Sea Series
Ships Ahoy
Rough Sea
High Tide

Lovers in London Series

Risking Millions
Venture Capital
Worth the Expense
The Price of Luxury
Exclusive Passion

Love You Series
Love Life
Need Love
My Love

Managing the Billionaire
Never Enough
Worth the Cost
Secret Admirers
Chasing Affection
Pressing Romance
Timeless Memories
Managing the Billionaire Box Set Books #1-3

Managing the Bosses Series
The Boss
The Boss Too
Who's the Boss Now
Love the Boss
I Do the Boss
Wife to the Boss
Employed by the Boss

Brother to the Boss
Senior Advisor to the Boss
Forever the Boss
Christmas With the Boss
Billionaire in Control
Billionaire Makes Millions
Billionaire at Work
Precious Little Thing
Priceless Love
Valentine Love
The Cost of Freedom
Trick or Treat
The Night Before Christmas
Gift for the Boss - Novella 3.5
Managing the Bosses Box Set #1-3
Managing the Bosses Novellas

Mislead by the Bad Boy Series
Deceived
Provoked
Betrayed

Model Mayhem Series
Shameless
Modesty
Imperfection

Moment in Time

Highlander's Bride
Victorian Bride
Modern Day Bride
A Royal Bride
Forever the Bride

Mountain Millionaire Series
Close to the Ridge
Crossing the Bluff
Climbing the Mount

My Best Friend's Sister
Hometown Calling
A Perfect Moment
Thrown in Together

My Darker Side Series
Darkest Hour
Time to Stop
Against the Light

Neverending Dream Series
Neverending Dream - Part 1
Neverending Dream - Part 2
Neverending Dream - Part 3
Neverending Dream - Part 4

Neverending Dream - Part 5
Neverending Dream Box Set Books #1-3

Outside the Octagon
Submit
Fight
Knockout

Protecting Diana Series
Her Bodyguard
Her Defender
Her Champion
Her Protector
Her Forever
Protecting Diana Box Set Books #1-3

Protecting Layla Series
His Mission
His Objective
His Devotion

Racing Hearts Series
Rush
Pace
Fast

Regency Romance Series
The Duchess Scandal - Part 1
The Duchess Scandal - Part 2

Reverse Harem Series
Primals
Archaic
Unitary

Roommate Wanted Series
The Roommate

R&S Rich and Single Series
Alex Reid
Parker
Sebastian

Saving Forever
Saving Forever - Part 1
Saving Forever - Part 2
Saving Forever - Part 3
Saving Forever - Part 4
Saving Forever - Part 5
Saving Forever - Part 6

Freedom Forever
Soldier's Fortune

Spanked Series
Passion
Playmate
Pleasure

Spelling Love Series
The Author
The Book Boyfriend
The Words of Love

Strength & Style
Suits You, Sir
Tailor Made
Perfect Gentleman

Taboo Wedding Series
He Loves Me Not
With This Ring
Happily Ever After

Tattooist Series
Confession of a Tattooist

Surrender of a Tattooist
Heart of a Tattooist
Hopes & Dreams of a Tattooist

Tennessee Romance
Whisky Lullaby
Whisky Melody
Whisky Harmony

The Bad Boy Alpha Club
Battle Lines - Part 1
Battle Lines

The Brush Of Love Series
Every Night
Every Day
Every Time
Every Way
Every Touch
The Brush of Love Series Box Set Books #1-3

The City of Mayhem Series
True Mayhem
Relentless Chaos
Broken Disorder

The Debt
The Debt: Part 1 - Damn Horse
The Debt: Complete Collection

The Fire Inside Series
Dare Me
Defy Me
Burn Me

The Gentleman's Club Series
Gambler
Player
Wager

The Golden Game
On The Pitch
Respect the Game
All Game
Sweat and Tears
The Final Score

The Golden Mail
Hot Off the Press
Extra! Extra!

Read All About It
Stop the Press
Breaking News
This Just In
The Golden Mail Box Set Books #1-3

The Lucky Billionaire Series
Lucky Break
Streak of Luck
Lucky in Love

The Millionaire's Pretty Woman Series
Perfect Stranger
Captive Devotion
Sweet Temptations

The Sound of Breaking Hearts Series
Disruption
Destroy
Devoted

The University of Gatica Series
The Recruiting Trip
Faster
Higher
Stronger

Dominate
No Rush
University of Gatica - The Complete Series

T.N.T. Series
Troubled Nate Thomas - Part 1
Troubled Nate Thomas - Part 2
Troubled Nate Thomas - Part 3

Toxic Touch Series
Noxious
Lethal
Willful
Tainted
Craved
Toxic Touch Box Set Books #1-3

Undercover Boss Series
Marketing
Finance
Legal

Undercover Series
Perfect For Me
Perfect For You
Perfect For Us

Unknown Identity Series
Unknown
Unpublished
Unexposed
Unsure
Unwritten
Unknown Identity Box Set: Books #1-3

Unlucky Series
Unlucky in Love
UnWanted
UnLoved Forever

War Torn Letters Series
My Sweetheart
My Darling
My Beloved

Wet & Wild Series
Stormy Love
Savage Love
Secure Love

Worth It Series

Worth Billions
Worth Every Cent
Worth More Than Money

You & Me - A Bad Boy Romance
Just Me
Touch Me
Kiss Me

Standalone
Wash
Loving Charity
Summer Lovin'
Love & College
Billionaire Heart
First Love
Frisky and Fun Romance Box Collection
Beating Hades' Bikers
Everyone Loves a Bad Boy
Dead of Night

Watch for more at www.lexytimms.com.

About the Author

"Love should be something that lasts forever, not is lost forever." Visit USA TODAY BESTSELLING AUTHOR, LEXY TIMMS https://www.facebook.com/SavingForever *Please feel free to connect with me and share your comments. I love connecting with my readers.* Sign up for news and updates and freebies - I like spoiling my readers! http://eepurl.com/9i0vD website: www.lexytimms.com Dealing in Antique Jewelry and hanging out with her awesome hubby and three kids, Lexy Timms loves writing in her free time. MANAGING THE BOSS-ES is a bestselling 10-part series dipping into the lives of Alex Reid and Jamie Connors. Can a secretary really fall for her billionaire boss?

Read more at www.lexytimms.com.